Mila Misses Mommy written by Judith Koppens and illustrated by Anouk Nijs

ISBN 978-1-60537-623-3

This book was printed in November 2020 at Wai Man Book Binding (China) Ltd.
Flat A, 9/F., Phase I, Kwun Tong Industrial Centre, 472-484 Kwun Tong Road, Kwun Tong, Kowloon, H.K.

First Edition
10 9 8 7 6 5 4 3 2 1

Written by Judith Koppens
Illustrated by Anouk Nijs

Mila

Misses Mommy

Clavis

NEW YORK

My name is Mila. Some days I live with my daddy and some days I live with my mommy. Today Mommy takes me to school. She has to leave right away. "See you later, Mila!" she says.

Liza sits at a table.
She's doing a beautiful puzzle.
"Will you join me?" she asks.
I sigh deeply. "I don't really feel
like doing puzzles today."

"Will you help me build a huge tower?"
Sen asks cheerfully.
"I don't really feel like building right now,"
I say softly.

The teacher claps her hands.
It's time to tidy up.
All eyes are on the teacher.
But I just stare at the floor.
I really don't feel like tidying up.

Britt and Sen put the snacks on the table.
It's almost time to eat. My tummy hurts,
I really don't feel like eating today.

"Aren't you hungry, Mila?" the teacher asks gently.
I shrug my shoulders. "My tummy hurts."
"Has your tummy hurt all morning?" the teacher asks.
"Not when I was with Mommy," I whisper.

The teacher understands.
"I think you miss your
mommy, Mila."
I nod, but I don't say
anything.

"I can understand," the teacher says.
"Everyone misses their mommy
now and then."
"Really?" I ask, full of surprise.

"Oh yes," the teacher says
as she takes my hand.
"Just come along with me."

"Sen and Liza, please listen," the teacher says. "Mila has a tummy ache, because she misses her mommy."

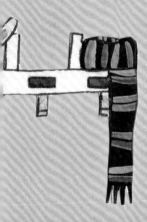

"Oh, that happened to me before!" Liza nods. "Why don't you play in the dress-up area for a while, so Mila can forget about her tummy ache?" the teacher asks.

"I want to be Mommy!" Liza calls out.
"Look, Mila! I'm putting on a dress that's
just like the one your mommy has."
I smile a little. Liza does look a bit like Mommy.

"Then I'll be your cat," Sen yells.
He wraps an orange cloth around his body.
I giggle. It's very funny to see.

"So you can be the child." Liza says, pointing at me. "We'll call you Mila, of course. You get hugs all the time." I like that!

I pet Sen the cat, and give Mommy Liza a big hug.
"Now I don't miss my mommy so much,"
I say with a big smile. "Thanks to you.
You're my best friends!"

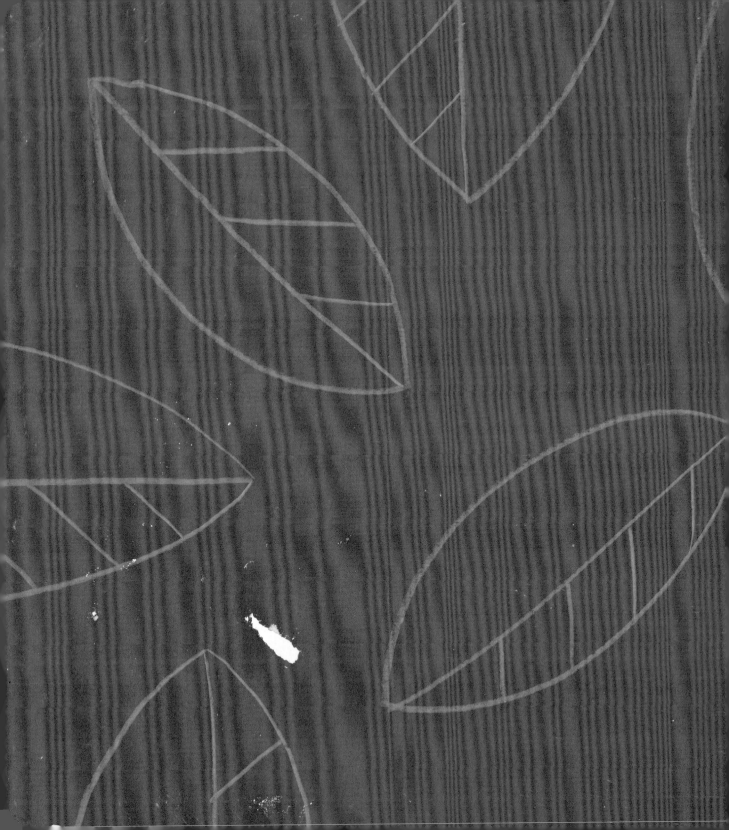